Floating Mind

Kuldeep Sharma

Ukiyoto Publishing

Acknowledgement

At the top of the list of acknowledgments, I would mention my grandfather, a folk poet, who passed on his genes to me. I am grateful to my parents, who introduced me to spirituality early by their high spiritual conduct.

Also, in this space, I would like to thank my wife and children, who inspired me to evolve as a writer in Hindi, English, and German. Last but not least, I thank my daughter, Daxita, who edited and proofread the manuscript of this book.

Contents

The human mind constantly fluctuates between the present, the past, and the future. In good times, it embarks on weaving happy dreams. In bad times, it goes to the past and remembers happy times, while it jumps to the future and thinks worrisome thoughts. Either way, it distracts us from reality, and as a result, we lose control of our thoughts and feelings, ultimately affecting our decision-making ability.

The following poems describe different moods of a floating mind. When it is restless, its thoughts are dominated by anxiety and fear. In a calm state, it is connected to the soul and generates thoughts of hope and courage.

Through these poems, the poet conveys that love is an innate quality of humankind which, however, is not let overwhelm life by the mind. Since the mind is fed with news of hunger, hatred, and conspiracies worldwide, it tends to miss the bliss of love that is the cure for all evil.

Courage

Even the strongest among us;
May suffer from anxiety and fear.
One may be overwhelmed;
Thinking a disaster is very near!

One may feel very low;
And may lose all hope.
The struggle has taken its toll;
Life has been on a descending slope!

Stop listening to naysayers;
Giving up is not a cure.
It's your dream, your journey;
Stay strong and endure!

Courage has magic;
And Faith has power.
Let's hang in there;
Fortune may smile any hour!

Character

Closed Minds
can never open new doors.

A Coward
can never roar.

A Pessimist
never finds new shores.

A Sadist
can never adore.

A Friend
will never abhor.

A Fighter
will always restore.

Omnipotent

You fall off the bed;
You never get up again.

You have a car crash;
You are crushed.

You slip into a coma;
Your life has a full stop.

Your boat capsizes;
You never resurface.

A step onto a nail;
You are nailed.

A snake bites you;
You bite the dust.

In fire,
You turn to ashes.

I can't resist believing;
You are the weakest living being!

Unreal

Pain and suffering are real;
Beyond boundaries is the ordeal.
Hurt are even the lungs of steel;
The whole world seems so unreal!

The numb mind can't feel;
We have lost hold of the wheel.
There is no joy to conceal;
I wish it were a world of a reel.

Nature has mysteries to reveal;
It has its own ways how to heal.
It knows how to deceive and deal;
Humanity will soon get back its zeal.

Timeline

Ignorance evaporates
Wisdom settles.

Time flies
Memories live.

Weeds die out
Flowers bloom.

People depart
Soulmates stay.

The clouds dwindle
The sun shines.

Struggle diminishes
Success is crowned.

Worries disappear
Happiness beckons.

Modesty

The rich are proud of their kingdom,
The learned are proud of their wisdom.

The honest are proud of their honesty,
The modest of their modesty.

The kind are proud of their kindness,
The healthy are proud of their wellness.

The saint is proud of his purity,
The philanthropist of his charity.

The winners are proud of their victory,
The old are proud of history.

The powerful are proud of their might,
The fighters are proud of their fight.

The lovers are proud of their love,
The believers are proud of the Gods above.

Let Go

If you love
Let go.
If you have expectations
You are inviting woe.

If someone hurt you
Let go.
If you don't
It will only grow.

If you have been cheated
Let go.
How they would pay
You shall never know.

If you have been used
Let go.
The souls are connected
It's a debt they owe.

Within

It's warm!
It's the warmth in my heart.

Let's talk.
Don't you understand my silence?

What perfume are you wearing?
It's the scent of my soul.

Vitamin E is good for the skin.
Meditation is nutritious for the soul.

You have good eyesight.
But not much of a vision.

Do you want Water?
I already have in my eyes.

Transitional

During your sunny days
You get addicted to praise.
The fortunes rise, time decays;
Life is just a passing phase.

During your rainy days
You feel you are in a cage.
The Sun has cruel rays;
Your best friend betrays.

Apathy, if the world displays;
Your faith you must raise
To buck up, find new ways:
Remove the smoke and haze.

Dream and persevere always;
Stay firm if your heart strays.
A stubborn mind the Gods gaze;
Success will be a dazzling blaze.

Daughter

When she is born;
She is like a living doll.
It's a sight to behold;
When you see her crawl.

While you hold her hand;
She grows to be a princess.
Tightly she holds your heart;
As she wears a pink dress.

Proudly watch mother and father;
She grows into a winsome lady.
Elegant, intelligent, and chubby
Gorgeous, she is still a baby.

She is her parents' best friend;
To her love, there's no end.
Unlimited support she will lend;
She can command stars to bend.

You are not here forever to stay;
Explore live and make your way.
Be healthy and happy, we pray;
Spread your wings and fly away.

Blessed

No need to stress
It doesn't make worries less.

You may be now under heavy duress
Don't let it hinder the desire to progress.

Control the thoughts that you possess
Trust nature's unique process.

Keep your spirits high in distress
It ruins your health if felt in excess.

It is all right if your life is in a mess
That's how failures turn into success.

Why do you think you are pressed?
Think instead that you are blessed.

Innate

I feel hungry.
I love.

I feel thirsty;
I love.

I need sleep.
I love.

I yearn to learn.
I love.

I am happy.
I love.

I bathe.
I love.

I am sad.
I love.

I cry.
I love.

Limitless

You could have been a famous singer!
I saw myself in Paul McCartney.

You could have been a successful writer!
I imagined Franz Kafka to be me!

You could have been a successful actor!
I thought Anthony Hopkins was me!

You could have created your own identity!
I didn't want to limit myself to myself!

Mortal

I live in my own house.
I pay the rent.

I get minor repairs done.
Plumber, carpenter, dentist.

I pay for water and electricity.
Food, water, and education.

I throw parties.
I meditate.

I leave behind the house.
The body.

Choice

You have no choice
but to go on.

And get past
the foggy dawn.

Hold your lazy yawn
let your future be drawn.

Look beyond
your narrow lawn.

You will find
the misery is gone!

Options

Getting stuck in traffic
Or speeding through life.

To crawl in the sky
Or to fly on the ground.

Climbing down
Or sliding up.

To die young
Or to be born old.

Celebrating death
Or mourning life.

To hate the body
Or to love the soul.

Unknown

I am a stranger here
And have come by chance.
I never left anything
To circumstance.

I didn't leave all to the stars;
Though I believe in my horoscope.
I kept my mind scientific
While walking on a tightrope.

I applied
Hard work and intelligence;
Didn't believe anything blindly;
Did all my due diligence.

I erred and succeeded;
I weighed and failed.

I celebrated;
I wailed.

Heritage

Please give me food.
India has a rich cultural heritage.

I have no job.
Let's run a marathon.

I have no roof over my head.
Let's go on a pilgrimage.

I will die.
May your soul find peace.

Reality

The soul is not visible.
Body is.

The heart is not visible.
Conduct is.

Thoughts are not evident.
Action is.

Feelings are not obvious.
Expressions are.

Intentions are not heard.
Words are.

Love is not loud.
Hatred is.

The Opposites

The hypocrites praise.
The honest criticize.

The opportunists run away.
The strong stay.

The optimists hope.
The pessimists dope.

The weak hate.
The strong love.

The wise challenge misfortune.
The ignorant embrace death.

Success

A thought you nurture;
Shapes your future.

Believe in your dream;
It may be a divine scheme.

The distance traveled;
Is the path leveled.

On the way, if you get tired;
Buck up and get inspired.

Each difficulty you conquer;
Makes you stronger.

If someone pulls you down;
You are getting the crown.

Remain a gentle and pure soul;
However high may be your goal.

Affirmations

I can't sleep these days.
I am sleeping like a baby.

I am not well.
I am at the gym.

I am scared of heights.
I am climbing a rock.

I have no money.
I am on holiday in the Bahamas.

My partner doesn't love me.
My partner pampers me so much!

I am a failure.
The world is applauding me.

The pandemic has been raging for long.
I am a healthy mind in a healthy body.

Luck

You have children.
Do you understand them?

You have a loving life partner.
Do you reciprocate?

You have a good family health history.
Don't you feel fortunate?

You are successful.
Aren't you grateful?

You are a self-made man!
Oh, Really?

Priorities

If people are on a leaving spree;
They are the leaves,
And you are the tree.

When you are laden with fruits;
People will come,
And throw at you boots.

Bend deep like grass;
Let them reject you,
Stand up again as they pass.

Enjoy, celebrate, and unwind;
Hold them tight,
True friends are hard to find.

Triumph

Calmness triumphs over Struggle.

Warmth defeats Apathy.

Smile conquers Sorrow.

Silence beats Noise.

Benevolence overpowers Greed.

Wisdom defeats Ignorance.

Faith silences Despair.

Love prevails over Hatred.

Life challenges Death.

You Shape Me

I am

The waves in the sea;

The water in the river;

The raindrop in the clouds;

The snow on the mountains;

The Stream in the hills;

The waterfall in the mountains;

The dew on the leaves;

The moisture in the air;

The sweat on the forehead;

The vapor in the breath;

The saliva in the kiss;

The tears in the eyes;

You shape me
I become.

Family

Let's pray for family and friends;

That their love ascends.

All evil and hate it fends;

Their love transcends all ends.

When this journey ends;

And I leave my family and friends;

I will make amends;

So that the bond never ends.

Whether we were foes or friends;

The story never ends.

Even if someone pretends;

No one knows when the road bends.

Our glory begins and ends;

A boon, such as family and friends.

A heart that a loved one lends;

That only a soulmate comprehends.

Despair

The injured pride never comes into tears;
The heart is not as hard as it appears.

From fear to hope and hope to fear;
Time has gone by year after year.

You see people with taunting stares;
Your misery has become amusement theirs.

The sorrow that chases you everywhere;
Don't let it become your worst nightmare.

With perseverance, belief, and prayer;
You will find the way out of despair.

Even the Sun waits for the clouds to clear;
Wait for your luck, which shall soon appear.

Alchemy

Stand up;
Awaken!
Love and live;
Smile and laugh!

Eat healthy;
Be kind to yourself always!
Practice yoga;
Don't be a thief of your peace!

Hang in there;
Don't lose heart!
Just let go,
Let your spirit float!

Be composed;
Sing a beautiful song!
Take a deep breath;
You are the creator of your destiny!

Meditate;
Ascend!
Have patience;
Never give up in life!

Keep on working;

Do not fear any pandemic!

Stay strong;

Thoughts are alchemic!

If They Could

If they could

the eyes see;

the ears hear;

the mind understand;

the hands touch;

the feet walk;

the nose breathe;

the tongue taste;

the heart feel;

And the soul speak!

Expect A Miracle

Emotions are energy carriers.
Fear creates a barrier.

Stay awake and never rest in peace.
Or else your problems will increase.

When you fail to raise your consciousness.
Take God's cognizance.

When things don't seem to fall in line.
Trust God's design.

Whether bliss or woe.
Go with the flow.

Don't be too cynical.
Always expect a miracle.

The Mask

As their feet are turning cold;
They have tightened the mold.

Their lies are repeated and cold;
The truth used to be made of gold.

They have the power to control;
We must do as we are told.

The mask is the new blindfold;
Democracy is on hold.

Impropriety

Because of curiosity
I'm just riddled with anxiety.

In a twisted society
We drown in anxiety.
Feel the feeding of my sanity

I see souls full of variety
Lit the spark to my anxiety.

What of propriety?
There are rules we obey in society.
I have no use for piety;
Or notions of propriety.

Discovery

Ginger Tea
is better than Green tea.

Home-cooked food
is delicious.

My daughter
has two new teeth.

My mother
has two teeth less.

We
have a new pet.

The view from our balcony
is beautiful.

Whiskey at home
tastes better than elsewhere.

I can still
do a headstand.

You Can

With closed eyes, you see;
With wide-open eyes, you don't.
You say nothing with words;
And say a lot in silence.

You are lovable but not loved;
You love but don't feel.
You eat food but don't know its taste.
You breathe but don't feel the breath.

You hear all, but your soul;
You travel but only outward.
You are victorious and know nothing;
You are a failure and are learned.

Sometimes, you walk;
And reach nowhere.
Sometimes, you just sit;
And still, reach.

Own Your Soul

In you resides a wandering soul;
Its journey is under nobody's control.

When you treat someone like a soul;
Love glows in your bosom like coal.

When you wander for your soul;
You fleet towards the final goal.

If you can control your thoughts' role;
You own your soul.

Disclosure

He is an old acquaintance
of mine.
A nice man.

Yesterday I broke into his house
and looked
for my name tag.

There were many drawers.
But on one of them
had my name on it.

I had the key with me
and I opened it.
I froze.

Nourish Your Soul

Accept diversity.

Be calm.

Be grateful.

Be humble.

Be optimistic.

Be patient.

Celebrate others' success.

Don't envy.

Eat light.

Enjoy romance.

Enjoy solitude.

Exercise.

Forgive.

Help others selflessly.

Let your ego starve.

Listen to music.

Live in the present.

Love.

Meditate.

Practice silence.

Read.

Respect others' viewpoints.

Smile.

Stop worrying.

Cause And Effect

If I am blessed
You are a blessing.
If I am happy
You are happiness.

If I love
You are love.
If I sing
You are the Song.

If I think
You are the thought.
If I fly
You are the Sky.

If I am alive
You are life.

Silence

Mind excels in silence.
Heart jells in silence.
Courage yells in silence.
Faith dwells in silence.
Love swells in silence.

Comparative

The arrogance of the wise is more dangerous
Than that of an ignorant.

The criticism by a loved one is more helpful
than by an adversary.

Hatred of a friend is more hazardous
than of an enemy.

Praise by an opponent is more genuine
than by a friend.

The treachery of an angel is more hurtful
than that of a demon.

An instant connection with a stranger is more divine
than any old relationship.

February

The best month of the year is February;

Just as out of all fruits is blueberry!

Valentine's and love come in a flurry;

This month is like a romance library!

It's shorter but truly very extraordinary;

The thoughts today are not momentary!!

Not too high not too low stands Mercury;

A perfect season to woo and marry!

Songstress

In the middle of a raging pandemic;
flowers are blooming in full swing.
There is agony and gloom is very thick;
The fear of death is engulfing everything.

Anxiety is endless, the heart as cold as clay;
But happiness will return and relieve the pain.
The remedies and blessings are on their way;
The songstress is waiting to sing again.

Celebrations

She flips through the photo album;
And reads greeting cards.
She has tears streaming down her cheeks.
Today is a holiday.

She stares at the phone.
But it remains silent.
Thoughtfully, she goes to the window.
And looks out.

The calm is frightening.
The sky is grey.
The bare branches of the trees tremble.
It looks like snow.

The cars yawn.
Their windows are covered with snow.
Two laborers are walking on the street.
She turns on the television.

With a worried face
She looks at the clock.
It is midnight.
She is tired.

Some candles are still burning.

It is dark.

The big Christmas tree stands in all its glory.

She lies down peacefully.

The Way Up

Good day.
Yes.
I will do it immediately.
Of course.

Hello.
How are you
You need not mention it.
I am grateful.

How is the family doing?
Nice tie!
It is for the little one.
I would be happy.

Good evening!
It goes without saying.
Ha ha ha.
My pleasure!

Affirmations

I can't sleep at the moment.
I sleep like a baby.

I am not feeling well.
I am in the gym.

I suffer from vertigo.
I am climbing a rock.

I don't have any money.
I am taking a vacation in the Bahamas.

My partner doesn't love me.
My partner spoils me so much!

I am a failure.
The world applauds me.

The pandemic has been raging for a long time.
I am a healthy mind in a healthy body.

Communication

I called you yesterday.
I guess you weren't there.

Yes, I wasn't there.
I went for a walk.

That was Sunday evening.
I thought you'd be home.

The weather was nice.
I thought I'd go for a walk.

I thought I had the wrong number.
Then I tried again.

I didn't go for a walk for a long time.
But this time, I did go.

I thought maybe you were in the bathroom.
But you weren't there.

I've been looking forward to it for a long time.
And the weather was good yesterday.

House Rules

Pets not allowed.

Pressure cooker with whistle prohibited.

Please play music softly.

Please laugh softly.

Children not allowed.

Never leave apartment door open.

Set the telephone and alarm at low volume.

Do not let the taps drip.

Do not drop anything on the floor.

Walk quietly in the corridor.

Stay quiet after 10 o'clock.

The Culprit

Grandpa!
What is a tree?

Hey.
Look at the picture here.

Beautiful!
Have you ever seen one?

Silly!
I have even felled one.

Hospitality

Please make yourself comfortable.

What would you like to drink?

I don't know if you will like it.

Please try it.

Why don't you have some of this too?

You have not tested it at all.

Please have some more.

Just the last one.

I guess you didn't like the food.

Cheers!

Enjoy your meal.

The Chatter

How is your new car running?
I have an old car.
Didn't you buy a new one?
No, my old one still runs just fine.

How is the baby doing?
Which baby?
Yours, of course!
But we're not expecting!

How did it go?
What?
The divorce.
But we're happily married.

Why did you quit your job?
Why would I do that?
I heard you were leaving!
None that I know of.

Gender Equality

I am just as ambitious
as he is.

I am just as educated
as he is.

I am just as capable
as he is.

I am as important
as he is.

I am just as selfish
as he is.

I am just as manly,
as he is.

About the Author

Kuldeep Sharma

Kuldeep Sharma is a lecturer of the German language. He taught German at the Goethe Institute in New Delhi (Max Mueller Bhavan) for 15 years. Previously, he worked for German Television in Germany.

He is a corporate master trainer and motivational speaker. In his self-help workshops, he blends modern methods with spiritual practice. He firmly believes we are spiritual beings, and our happiness lies in being in synch with nature, disposing of outdated ideas, misconceptions, and beliefs about life. Spirituality is a process of finding the self and expanding the horizon of consciousness.

Kuldeep Sharma has had life experiences beyond usual scientific understanding. He was exposed to spirituality early and blessed with the gift of premonition. He has been writing poems, plays, short stories, and words of wisdom in Hindi, English, and German for a long time. He has been on editorial boards of several educational intuitions. He has already published two books, 'Movement In Moments' and 'Rachiyata Se Rachna Tak' (the creator and the creation).

9 789360 169831